Wild

Dreamers

ALSO BY MARGARITA ENGLE

* also available in Spanish

* *Enchanted Air:*
Two Cultures, Two Wings: A Memoir

The Firefly Letters:
A Suffragette's Journey to Cuba

* *Forest World*

Hurricane Dancers:
The First Caribbean Pirate Shipwreck

Jazz Owls
A Novel of the Zoot Suit Riots

The Lightning Dreamer:
Cuba's Greatest Abolitionist

* *Lion Island:*
Cuba's Warrior of Words

The Poet Slave of Cuba:
A Biography of Juan Francisco Manzano

* *Rima's Rebellion:*
Courage in a Time of Tyranny

Silver People:
Voices from the Panama Canal

* *Soaring Earth:*
A Companion Memoir to Enchanted Air

* *The Surrender Tree:*
Poems of Cuba's Struggle for Freedom

Tropical Secrets:
Holocaust Refugees in Cuba

The Wild Book

* *Wings in the Wild*

* *With a Star in My Hand:*
Rubén Darío, Poetry Hero

* *Your Heart, My Sky:*
Love in a Time of Hunger

Wild Dreamers

MARGARITA ENGLE

atheneum

New York London Toronto Sydney New Delhi

An imprint of Simon & Schuster Children's Publishing Division
1230 Avenue of the Americas, New York, New York 10020

Simon & Schuster: Celebrating 100 Years of Publishing in 2024
For information about special discounts for bulk purchases, please contact Simon & Schuster Special Sales at 1-866-506-1949 or business@simonandschuster.com.
The Simon & Schuster Speakers Bureau can bring authors to your live event. For more information or to book an event, contact the Simon & Schuster Speakers Bureau at 1-866-248-3049 or visit our website at www.simonspeakers.com.
Interior design by Rebecca Syracuse
The text for this book was set in Charter Roman.
Manufactured in the United States of America
First Edition
10 9 8 7 6 5 4 3 2 1

Library of Congress Cataloging-in-Publication Data
Names: Engle, Margarita, author.
Title: Wild dreamers / Margarita Engle.
Description: First edition. | New York : Atheneum Books for Young Readers, 2024. | Audience: Ages 12 and Up. | Summary: Told in alternating voices, determined to make a difference and heal from their troubled pasts, teens Ana and Leandro fight to protect California wildlife and the endangered puma.
Identifiers: LCCN 2023005405 | ISBN 9781665939751 (hardcover) | ISBN 9781665939775 (ebook)
Subjects: CYAC: Novels in verse. | Family problems—Fiction. | Anxiety—Fiction. | Wildlife conservation—Fiction. | Puma—Fiction. | Cat family (Mammals)—Fiction. | California—Fiction. | Cuban Americans—Fiction. | LCGFT: Novels in verse. | Romance fiction.
Classification: LCC PZ7.5.E54 Wic 2024 | DDC [Fic]—dc23
LC record available at https://lccn.loc.gov/2023005405

for scientists
and future scientists
with gratitude, admiration, and hope

REWILDING is a conservation practice that restores natural habitats. It includes establishing wildlife crossings and the protection of apex predators. Wildlife crossings allow animals to safely cross highways and other human-made barriers. These crossings prevent the genetic isolation of breeding populations. Apex predators are at the top of the food chain, with no predators of their own, although they are vulnerable to hunting, habitat loss, and other harmful actions by humans.

RAFTER

Leandro

age 17

My family fled Cuba
on a lashed-together jumble
of inner tubes, balsa wood, and fear
exactly ten years ago, when I had just learned
how to read, and all I craved were tales
of adventure.

At sea on la balsa, my own true story
became terrifying in a way
that makes memory
dangerous.

First there was a hidden cavern
where a mysterious couple
known as Amado and Liana
were surrounded by singing dogs
and cave paintings of a bird-girl
serenaded by a young man
with an enchanted guitar
that is said to attract
winged and four-legged creatures
who love melodies the same way
bird-girl and guitar-boy
love each other.

Musical dogs and magical songs
were enough to send my imagination swirling
like dough in a mixing bowl at the bakery,
but there would be no fresh bread
or sweet pastelitos
on that perilous raft
where I lost
all courage.

Liana gave us canned food, bottled water,
and a compass, while Amado crafted sun-hued
life jackets of yellow nylon stuffed with silky fluff
from the seedpods of a sacred ceiba tree.

On a moonless midnight, la balsa was set afloat,
and soon my parents, my older brother, Emilio, and I
were all trembling in the sway of massive waves
as we reeled beyond wheeling circles of sharks
beneath streamers of migrating
butterflies
and hummingbirds.

I told myself that if fragile winged animals
could be brave

above those waves
so could I, but instead of courage
all I discovered
was horror
followed by sorrow
and then the mercy
of a stowaway blue merle puppy
who knew how to offer comfort
by singing wordless canine melodies
that are even more powerful
than the ocean.

Cielo the singing dog

I sang to the younger boy
because he was the one
who needed to be saved
from his own ragged
rhythm
of fear

NOCTURNAL
Leandro

It was my fault
that we were forced to flee our homeland.
It was my fault that Papi drowned
while saving me from
sinking.

I was the one who'd revealed my parents' secret
while we were still in Cuba, and I was the one
who fell off the raft and needed to be rescued.

I've been nocturnal ever since, kept awake
by nightmares of monstrous waves, eerie dreams
that stay with me throughout the next day
transformed into panic attacks.

Until the stowaway puppy was trained
to be my therapy dog, I fainted in water
and on land.

Cielo taught me to breathe
like a canine.

Cielo the singing dog

I hum a song
into his hand
until he understands
that it's time to sit
and stay still
so that if he faints
in the presence
of waves—either real
or imagined—he won't
forget how to inhale
slow
deep
restful
animal
music

THE WILD PARK

Ana

age 17

I feel like an island
in a sea of green leaves.

My bed is the back seat of our small
cluttered car, parked under huge trees.

What Mom and I really need
is a roof and walls, a floor,
and normal
sleep,
but here I am unhoused and awake,
so I dance along a dirt path beneath oaks
with branches that bend down like friends
who are eager to listen to the percussion
of my furiously
drumming
feet.

Unsheltered

Ana

This feral park is just one link
in a long chain of rewilded military outposts
called the Golden Gate National Recreation Area.

It's an urban wilderness, a long narrow green belt
that prevents development, keeping wildlife safe.

If only there were enough homes for people, too,
families like mine, with a hardworking mom
who can't even afford to rent a converted garage
this close to luxurious Silicon Valley,
where even the tiniest studio apartment
costs a fortune.

Mom almost makes enough money
as a government botanist
at the San Francisco airport,
where she identifies smuggled herbs
and rare orchids trafficked by greedy crooks
who import endangered species,
but most of her salary is gobbled
by all the expensive lawyers
and private detectives

she hired
in an effort to locate
my runaway dad . . .

so now the wild park is our outdoor home,
and all I can do is dance beneath oak trees
and wish
pray
believe
that somehow
there can be safe zones
for both—wild creatures
and houseless
humans.

FLOWER BUTTERFLY

Ana

At school I sit through classes
feeling like a topiary shrub
       trimmed
     and shaped
    by time
  so that no branch
is ever free to blossom.

Instead of listening to math formulas,
I reminisce about a century I'll never see
when my Ciboney Taíno namesake—Ana Tanamá—
was alive, arguing courageously in colonial courts,
a doomed effort to defend our tribal land
from the sharp swords and false documents
of los conquistadores.

"Ana Tanamá" means "Flower Butterfly" in Taíno.
I love to think of us as close relatives even though
she was born in 1555, the earliest ancestor
on my mother's ornately written family tree,
where I am the final line.

DIVERSITY

Ana

I don't speak up in social studies class
when we talk about a multicultural society.

Mom left Cuba by being lucky when she won el bombo,
the big drum, a random lottery, the most coveted
and almost impossible pathway to reach
these divided   but supposedly united
states.

Washington, DC, calls the lottery their
Diversity Immigration Visa Program,
but there aren't any fancy euphemisms
for the way this public school
is nearly all Latino,
while the children of tech workers
attend elite prep academies
that perpetuate California's
modern version
of segregation.

You can tell by the style of the fences.
Private schools resemble country clubs.
Public ones look like prisons.

DANCING WITH ANCESTORS
Ana

After another confusing school day
I run through the night-dark wild park,
moving through shimmering pools
of moonlight,
where shadows
beneath oak trees
soothe me
with lyrics
whispered
by leaves.

I imagine spirits celebrating
all around me—Ana Tanamá
and my other invisible relatives.

Their Taíno words are beautiful.
"Bohío" means "house," my favorite daydream.
"Cuyo" is "light," "güey" is "sun," "guatu" is "fire,"
"hura" means "wind," "huracán" is "storm,"
and "catey" is "trouble."

When I join the mystical dance
I feel my hopes rising toward turey,

the wide sky where everything
is blue and peaceful
so that maybe there's a way
to believe in apito—infinity,
a place I can reach
someday
only by surviving
now.

MOONLIT

Ana

Euphoric with dance-joy,
I pass signs that remind me to watch out
for rattlesnakes and poison oak, followed by
a warning that makes my heart gallop—
MOUNTAIN LION TERRITORY
IF YOU SEE A PUMA, TRY TO APPEAR LARGE.
REACH HIGH. SHAKE YOUR ARMS. MAKE NOISE.
BACK AWAY SLOWLY. NEVER RUN.

In other words, convince the predator
that I'm powerful too, not just a delicious
morsel of prey. . . .

But before I can even begin
to practice appearing LARGE,
I hear the most beautifully eerie
nonhuman melody,
as if moonlight
has been transformed
into music.

Cielo the singing dog

the girl absorbs my voice
and knows she's not alone
in this scented world
always circled
by a chorus
of musical growth

she is so clearly the boy's scent match
but how will I manage to show her
that he's so much more courageous
than he seems?

matchmaking is every singing dog's
greatest challenge
and most satisfying task

those who call us guardian angels don't realize
how hard we work to bring lovelight
into the stubborn realm
of short-nosed human
possibilities

THE FERAL GIRL
Leandro

Cielo sees her first, alerting me with a song
as if the girl were a danger, but this dancing vision
isn't scary, just graceful
and spectacular, her dark hair cascading
as she reaches up
to wave both arms,
fingers pointing
beyond
me,
until both Cielo and I turn
to face an adult male puma
who must weigh at least
two hundred pounds.

His eyeshine is amber,
reflecting moonlight.

Tawny muscles.
Unsheathed claws.
Exposed teeth.
A snarl.
He's ready to pounce
until the girl rears up and roars

a bilingual fury of curse words
that make her sound
just as cubana
as any old drunk lady
at a bus stop in Miami.

I smile.
She frowns.
Cielo serenades us.

Puma concolor, the girl says, naming
the wildcat by its scientific names,
both genus and species,
so I know
she's a nerd.

I MAKE MYSELF GROW
Ana

Hot guy.
Enchanting smile.
Cute blue merle dog.
Puma concolor.

I obey the sign's instructions
to make myself LARGE, easy enough
when I dance, arms reaching,
imaginary maracas shaking,
no matter that none of this
can be real. I must have fallen
asleep
in the car,
then plummeted
farther
and
farther
into my own weirdly
vivid dream world.

WE STUDY EACH OTHER

Leandro   *Ana*

her forest eyes   his warm gaze
green and brown   cedar skin
at the same time   sunrise smile

                  midnight hair

curvy   sturdy

    lively   steady

              while we stare
                 at each other
       the puma   disappears

          all these visions seem
                completely
                  unreal

WE STARTLE EACH OTHER
Leandro

Cielo is quiet and calm.
I bend down
to stroke soft blue fur,
        but the feral girl reaches
        at exactly the same moment.

Her dark hair
billows like a waterfall
made of shadows
until
here,
where our hands touch
on my dog's shoulder,
     my fingers
        glow
           hers, too,
               as if we're both
          moon-beings
         luminous.

Life Is a Question Mark

Ana

I back away slowly
just like the sign instructs
then I drift toward my car-bed
          hoping the sweet dog's
          beautiful boy
          doesn't see
          where
          I live
without a home
minerals in my bones
moonlight on my hands
everything is alive
even

air

AFTERIMAGE
Leandro

Cielo and I glide downhill
in the new bakery delivery van
on a winding country road
while that nameless
                        burst of light
stays with me—
the feral girl's forest eyes
gleaming like these streaks
                        of visible energy
            that shine
on my fingertips
            as I grip
the steering wheel,
struggling to cling
            to improbable
                        possibilities.

WHY?

Leandro

The bakery is empty.
Everyone must be asleep upstairs,
so I slip past a door to Tío Leno's flat
on the second floor
and ours on the third,
then up another set
of wooden steps
to a widow's walk
on the Victorian rooftop,
where Cielo hums with contentment
as I inhale salty air from the enormous ocean
far below, where whales leap and sing
in their own language.

If I tell myself that I'm brave,
will the lie turn into a truth?

Why didn't I speak boldly, ask the girl's name
or any other clue to the mystery
of our shared
                    radiance?

Cielo the singing dog

each song is an echo
of the ones before and after

but every melody of love
is always
new

and why makes no difference
only when—now

SCHOOL DAY BLUES
Ana

The hot guy with the blue dog
still seems eerily close,
almost as if our glow
is a memory,
not a daydream.

If only I could keep dancing
in that wild park
until I find him
again
and again
just like the ancestors
who never abandon me . . .

but instead, I perform
rehearsed motions all day, in every class
and at my locker, just casually pretending
that I'm not unhoused
and gloomy.

THE WRITTEN HISTORY OF TEENAGE GIRLS

Ana

In biology class
I work on my complicated lab project,
trying to make authentic black ink
from oak galls by extracting tannin
from clumps of inner bark
and outer wood that I gathered
in the wild park.

Galls are lumps created by wasps
infesting the trees.

There was a time when oak galls
were the primary source of ink for books,
newspapers, and letters.

Imagine the past without those clever insects—
there would hardly be any love notes at all,
just carved hearts on tree trunks
and secret wishes
like my own.

The School Counselor Knows

Ana

She can tell by my unwashed clothes
and sleepless gaze.

She advises me to always say "unhoused"
instead of "homeless," so I'll know it's temporary
and not an intrinsic aspect of my character,
but I'm pretty sure that when she drives away
at the end of each day, she returns to a place
that makes her feel homeful,
not just housed.

She gives me a gift—*The Book of Hope*
by Jane Goodall, Douglas Abrams, and Gail Hudson,
about protecting endangered species.

Then she leads me into a closet
filled with snacks, jackets, notebooks,
pencils, soap, toothpaste, tampons,
and other donated survival supplies
for students like me—kids
with hardworking
immigrant parents
who can't afford rent.

Everything is available
in this storage room of gifts
from rich strangers—everything
except dignity.

SEARCH

Leandro

I return to the park with Cielo,
hoping to find the feral girl,
but all we see is a coyote,
rabbits, owls, and a slimy
neon-yellow banana slug
that looks like a creature
from a science fiction movie.

Tomorrow I'll start a new school
with Cielo at my side—no one
can turn a service dog away,
not when she wears the vest
that looks like smooth cloth armor,
allowing her to protect me
from my otherwise
uncontrollable
               attacks
                        of
          dizzy
                    panic.

HOMEFUL

Ana

Mom looks younger tonight
as we sit in the car, munching crackers
and trail mix that I brought from
that storage room at school and pretzels
that she pilfered from the airport.

Tomorrow we'll move, Mom announces
in a cheerful voice that warms me.
She's changing jobs, accepting an offer
from a childhood friend.

She'll be managing a nursery.
Native California plants.
Milkweed for monarch butterflies.
Wild buckwheat to feed bumblebees.
Elderberries to attract songbirds.
Wild lilac for beauty and fragrance.

A childhood friend?
That means someone from Cuba.
A native plant nursery?
That will be physical labor
instead of politely listening to rage

about delayed planes, lost luggage,
flight cancellations, and plants confiscated
because they're a protected species or because
they might introduce crop pests and diseases.

When I ask my gleeful mother
where we'll park the car at night,
she actually giggles like a little girl,
thrilled to inform me
that her new job
comes with a cottage!

We won't be unhoused
or hopeless, we'll be homeful.

I glance down at my hands,
hoping they'll glow again
but apparently touching
a certain dog-walking boy
is the only way to create
that dreamlike
radiance.

I Dream with You
Leandro

Sueño contigo
whoever you are.

Why didn't I ask for a name,
number, address, any clue to your
identity . . . ?

Now you seem as impossible
as a gold-eyed puma after it vanishes
into darkness.

Asleep and awake
sueño contigo
constantly.

Do you ever dream
with me?

Salvaged

Ana

I walk through the last day
at my old school
knowing that ancestors
                    danced me
into this strange world
                    courageously.

Soon I'll be living in a cottage
where I won't have to fashion a makeshift bed
by stuffing clothes into a plastic trash bag.

There will be walls, a roof, maybe even bookshelves,
and the local population of unhoused people
will plummet from tens of thousands
to tens of thousands
minus two.

Mom and I can start eating at a table,
and we'll never forget to share
whatever we have
whenever a beggar
holds out a cupped hand

on a foggy night
as if patiently waiting
for a splash
  of sunlight.

First Day

Leandro

This new school's mascot is a snarling puma,
but the sports team logo says "cougar."

Mountain lion.
Catamount.
Panther.
Painter.
So many names for a species that ranges
all the way from Alaska to Patagonia.

When Cielo and I walk into biology class,
her service dog vest marks the two of us
as a six-legged, dual-hearted curiosity.
She's the size of a border collie
and just as smart and fuzzy, so girls
immediately coo and ask to pet her,
but I have to tell them it's not allowed.
Working dogs need to focus.
They can't play with strangers.

So I make an effort to meet amused gazes.
I'm determined to seem confident

even if no one understands my anxiety attacks
and the medical need for a canine companion . . .

but my veins suddenly churn,
then flow in slow motion
when I see the feral girl
from the wild park
calmly scribbling
some sort of archaic calligraphy
by dipping a long white feather
into a blue glass inkwell.

Are we studying time travel,
or is she really as unusual
as she seems?

CROWN SHY

Ana

He doesn't smile
and I can't manage to speak.

Maybe we're just crown shy
like forest trees that give each other's
upper branches
                        space

instead of
                        overlapping

so that most of the leaves
                receive at least a little bit
                                of sunlight.

I try to curve my lips, but the forced grin
feels as stiff as a frown.

I state my name out loud—Ana Tanamá—
while I wonder, will the blue dog's boy and I
                ever be bioluminescent again?

SIDE BY SIDE

Ana   *Leandro*

We walk	we don't talk
out of class	
together	

I reach	without a dog this would be
just to test	so awkward, but Cielo sings
the effect	
of touch	
it happens	skin glows
our hands	
gleam	
meteors	fireflies

      soar

Cielo the singing dog

with lovelight
even shadows
become as bright
as sunrise

First Conversation

Ana

We eat lunch together
mostly talking about Cielo,
the wild park, pumas, and the way
this school is only fifty percent brown,
mostly mexicanos but plenty of peruanos,
guatemaltecos, and salvadoreños,
families of fishermen, farmworkers,
whale watching guides, and surfers.
The only cubanos in this town
are right here at our table
and inside our houses.

It feels so amazing to say the word "casa"
followed by "home," as we switch back and forth,
testing all four of our shared languages,
English, Spanglish, Spanish, and a bit of Taíno,
along with the wordless allure of attraction,
as we continue to confess who we are,
where we've lived, why we moved,
family complications, relatives
left behind on the island
añoranza
esperanza

his brother
who wants to be a big-wave surfer
like his uncle, and my mother who
has a cool new job, and his father
who drowned while rescuing him,
and mine
who tossed
our family away
like trash.

When he leans close
his aroma is an enticing blend
of strong coffee
and cookie dough.

I wonder if I still smell unhoused
now that I'm homeful.

GLEAM

Leandro

I know it might sound like I'm bragging,
but I tell Ana about the rewilding club
at my old school in Miami and the project
I joined with Cielo, training her to follow
scent trails of tracks and scat
so we could help biologists map
parts of the Everglades where wildlife crossings
now protect the world's last two hundred
critically endangered Florida panthers,
whose main cause of death
is speeding traffic.

Ana agrees that rewilding is necessary.
Without predators, there is no balance.
Deer stop moving.
When they stay still
they eat all the tree seedlings
in one place, so that forests
gradually vanish, and the entire
landscape changes.

I'm proud of my dog's conservation work.
Ana responds by praising Cielo and then looking

right into me, as if she's just discovered
a wordless language
that flashes
and sparkles
like our hands.

EYE CONTACT

Ana

It's a detail they forgot to include
on that mountain lion warning sign in the wild park,
but I was unhoused long enough to know
that feline predators attack when you turn away,
while humans become more dangerous
if you stare.

Mom has always warned me
to never make eye contact with any man
for more than three seconds . . .

but I'm certain that Leandro is different.
The longer we gaze into each other's daydreams,
the more secure I feel, immersed
in gentleness.

Trust

Leandro

I can't believe I'm telling her things
I've never confessed to any friend
or counselor.

I start with the secret I revealed to a teacher
when I was seven, about the way Papi knew
that a corrupt Cuban government official
was selling all the good flour to fancy
hotel restaurants, while reserving
maggot-infested leftovers
for family bakeries like ours.
I thought la maestra would protect us,
but instead she reported Papi for supposedly
spreading false rumors, so that in the end
we were the ones who had to flee
on that raft.

If we'd stayed on the island, my father
would have died in prison, instead of
deep in the seafloor's loneliest
layers of sand.

WAVE AFTER WAVE

Ana

His story is so horrible
that I don't know what to say.

All I can offer is a streak of light
on his arm, as I brush it with my fingers.

Why did his family leave Miami? Why now?
He answers quietly, explaining that his mother
and her brother both nearly died of Covid,
but she was in Florida and her brother was here
in California, so now they've decided
to live all together, in a building
purchased by the uncle's
big-wave surfing championships
and sponsorships and by tech stocks
his tío bought so profitably
that there's no need for caution
when it comes to opening
a new bakery.

SECRETIVE

Leandro

I don't tell her that my older brother
is a big-wave surfer too, and that my uncle
wants to coach him, and that both
are fearless when they speak with awe
about Mavericks,

           the world-famous
winter swell

           only a mile off-shore,
where it will haunt me

           each night, even though
I can't see or hear those massive waves

           above the sound
of my own

           pounding heart.

I don't try to explain that my dog alerts me
every time the scent of fight-or-flight adrenaline
builds up to such a dangerous level that I might
faint, fall, hit my head, and suffer one more
concussion, all that panic induced by nothing
but the memory of water's weight.

FLOATING

Ana

After school I can't find Leandro and Cielo,
so I walk away alone, thrilled with the knowledge
that I have a cottage to walk toward, and a friend
to talk with at lunchtime, and a source
of light that defies all the laws of physics,
springing from deep inside my hands
instead of the surface, where skin
is opaque.

I feel like I'm adrift in midair
even though my feet are solid,
and I can hear their strength
pounding hard earth
as I drum my way
dance-like
toward
home
while above me
seagulls circle and pelicans soar.

FRAGRANCE

Ana

Wild Rosa's Native Plant Nursery
smells like a wilderness of moist soil
and photosynthesis.

Mom is busy watering potted redwoods, fir, spruce,
incense cedar, cypress, oaks, pines, sycamores, willows,
alders, laurel bay, toyon, and brilliant red-barked
manzanita and madrón,
with peeling branches
that resemble cinnamon.

Smaller pots hold sage, wild roses, paintbrush,
lupines, yerba buena, and other aromatic blossoms
where bees and hummingbirds hover.

The cottage is a haven—two bedrooms
and a sunporch overflowing
with tropical palms, orchids, air plants. . . .

Where did the nursery's name come from?
Did Mom's childhood friend call it Wild Rosa
in her honor, and when was she ever wild?

THE SISTER OF MOM'S CHILDHOOD FRIEND

Ana

She's sweet like her name—Dulce.
She hugs me as if she's known me
all her life.

Dulce helps me get settled, shows me how
to care for orchids and bromeliads
in the greenhouse-porch that creates
an illusion of the tropics, but on this foggy coast
brightness isn't dependable, so special bulbs
in all the light fixtures imitate sunrays.

Dulce says her brother bought the nursery
so he could help my mother, an act of generosity
that makes no sense, unless—ah, no matter,
if this mystery man is more than a friend
at least Mom will be happier than she was with Dad.

The scent of green growth helps me feel free
and sheltered at the same time, like a forest bird
or a butterfly that has just emerged from the slow
seemingly impossible process of metamorphosis.

My Fugitive Father

Ana

Dad is an ABC—American-born Cuban
like I am. He grew up in Miami and became
a pilot, just so he could rescue rafters lost at sea
as they attempted to flee la isla,
but somewhere along the way
he listened to extremists,
absorbed conspiracy theories,
and chose to believe that Mom and I
are the ones who don't understand
science and history.

He thinks vaccines
carry tracking chips.

He's convinced that climate change
is a myth, and species aren't in danger
of extinction, and racism isn't real.

The last time I saw Dad was two years ago,
when he joined a militia training camp
armed with weapons of war.

When Dad left, he stole our identities,
both Mom's and mine—social security numbers

so he could get fake credit cards
that broke our hearts
and closed
our bank accounts.

Now he's on the FBI's most-wanted list
for domestic terrorism, the result of bombs
and other
secrets.

UNPACKING
Ana

Alone on the sunporch, I empty boxes
retrieved from storage—old photo albums,
the family tree, las maracas, a Taíno dictionary,
and books, all my childhood favorites about animals
and nature, and this new one that I received
from that counselor
at my last school.

I leaf through the pages,
rereading passages by Jane Goodall
about hope as a science with goals, pathways,
confidence, and support—four skills
that can be studied, just like biology
or any other
factual wonder . . .

but if hope is a science,
then I must be an experiment.

SUNROOM

Leandro

When I learn that Ana is the daughter
of Tío Leno's new nursery manager,
I drive to the cottage to invite them
to the bakery's grand opening
just in case Mami forgot
to be hospitable.

No one answers the front door,
but around back, I see Ana in a glass room
with sky-blue curtains pulled wide open.

She's dancing alone, shaking maracas
while reading a book, a combination
of activities that doesn't seem possible,
but everything else about her seems
just as unlikely, so I tell Cielo to sing,
and soon we're both invited into a nest
of palms, ferns, and flowers
that smell like Cuba.

There's a hammock and blankets
that make it look like someone plans
to sleep here, or at least take a siesta.

Ana is surrounded by books.
I long to make eye contact, but I force
my gaze down toward titles, so I won't
alarm her with my intense
attraction.

Around the World in 80 Trees
by Jonathan Drori

The Radiant Lives of Animals
by Linda Hogan

World of Wonders
by Aimee Nezhukumatathil

Half-Earth
by Edward O. Wilson

With Cielo's help, I manage to smile
and speak about biology class, hoping
that when I pick up *Half-Earth*
Ana will see that I'm not trying
to overwhelm her with attention.

It's a devastating book, essential and true,
because if we don't rewild half of Earth,
we'll lose biodiversity, millions of species
gone forever . . .

but I refuse to feel discouraged today,
so I keep reading titles, poetry books
by Dulce María Loynaz, Gabriela Mistral,
Joy Harjo, and Mary Oliver, all women,
all brilliant, just like the sun that streams
in around us,
reminding me
that in that wild park
and at school today
one touch was enough
to flood my brain
with radiance.

FINGERTIPS

Ana

Leandro asks to borrow *The Book of Hope*.
I'm glad, because it means he'll have to
come back
to return it.

When he invites me to the grand opening
of a bakery named Dulce's, meaning Sweet's,
I begin to understand that it's his mother's name
and that his uncle must be Mom's childhood friend.

Before he leaves, he lifts one hand
to caress my cheek with his fingers,
and even without glancing at a mirror
I know my face
is now a sunray.

So I do the same,
and his smile accepts
my light.

Visible

Ana

I don't know how my ancestors spelled their word
for hand, but it's usually shown as "ajápu" now
in modern Taíno dictionaries and textbooks,
with a Spanish *j* pronounced like an English *h*.

Hands are one of the shapes that appear on cave walls
all over the western Caribbean islands, where los Taíno
lived illuminated by the music of las maracas,
so after Leandro leaves with Cielo
I dance alone,
waving my fingers
to show the remnants
of our glow
to my invisible
companions.

My Mother's Love Story
Ana

In the morning I ask Mom about Leandro's tío.
As usual, any tale told by an adult turns out to be
complicated and intricate, with surprising twists.

Mom and Leno grew up together as best friends,
then fell in love while studying botany in Havana,
but he disappeared, so she applied for the US
immigration lottery
and won.

Recently, they ran into each other at the airport,
where he told her he vanished only because he
was in prison, arrested for making surfboards
at a time when surfing was forbidden
because it was so easy
to add a motor
and transform
a board
into
a boat.

While Leno was imprisoned,
no communication was allowed,

so he had no way to tell his girlfriend
that he was alive . . .

but as soon as he was released,
he followed her to Florida, windsurfing
all the way
from the island,
a journey so long
and exhausting
that he spent a week
in a hospital before he could begin
his desperate search.

By the time Leno found Rosa in Miami,
she was already married and I was three,
a happy child whose life Mom refused
to disrupt.

Leno moved to California, and he's been here
surfing Mavericks
all these years.

SPARK

Ana

Mom says she doesn't know what's next.
For now she and Leno are just friends.

I understand, because when I wonder about Leandro,
my answers multiply like kaleidoscope sections,
spinning and changing, depending on the angle.

Crush
or infatuation?
Lovelight at first sight
or just wishful twinkles?

How am I supposed to choose only one answer
to a question with so many glittering facets?

All I know is that there's a glow between us.
We flare up inside like sunlit prisms, a brightness
that flows through the skin
and can't be
ignored.

Cielo the singing dog

wave
particle
fragrance
no canine
wisdom
can ever
define
love's
light

and yet
singing dogs still constantly strive
to be loyal matchmakers for humans
whose noses are useless
for locating
scent mates

ABRAZOS
Leandro

Dulce's Cuban Bakery is ready
for the grand opening!

Every sweet and savory delicacy
is on display in glass cases.

I baked dozens of little abrazos—cookie hugs—
with wrapped tips like an embrace, the insides
stuffed with chocolate, dulce de leche,
queso crema, or guayaba.

I made empanadas and pastelitos
with a variety of fruit or meat fillings
and the small, cone-shaped coffee cakes
we call cappuccinos, and mini-churros
with all sorts of sauces for dipping,
and bite-sized coquitos, little balls
of soft, chewy coconut.

Mami made the big cakes
and fruity cheesecakes
and crusty pan cubano
in memory of Papi's
fresh bread.

Emilio and Leno stirred all the flan
and other puddings of sweet potatoes, natilla,
and dulce de leche made the authentic way:
slowly caramelized milk,
not the condensed version
from a can.

Croquetas, torticas, pastel de tres leches,
and pineapple cakes, there are so many
traditional snacks, treats, and pastries
that every Caribbean in the San Francisco Bay Area
is sure to show up, along with all Leno's friends—
big-wave champions, children from surf camps,
and gardeners who love the nursery
where right now Ana is probably
waking up hungry.

Should I hug her when she walks in
or just offer a cookie with the name "abrazos"
as a symbol?

WINGS

Leandro

Blue dress, fluttery skirt
shimmers
ripples
shy
smile

ready
to hug me or flee
depending on what I do next
so I wait and let her be the one
who decides whether to stay or fly.

CAFECITO

Ana

I sit on the patio of the bakery
while Mami is inside with Leno.
They're so sweet together.
How weird would it be if they end up
falling in love all over again, after
so many years?

Leandro waves, but he's busy.
If the espresso is strong, that's all I need.
I can't let myself gobble too many of these
fragrant Cuban sweets that will make me crave more
and more azúcar.

Maybe it should be the same with relationships.
Caution, not frenzy.
If I really let myself fall for Leandro,
how will I ever
climb back up toward independence?

When he finally has a free moment,
he brings me a sampler plate and a tiny cup
of the most powerful café cubano I've ever tasted,
even richer and darker than coffee in Miami.

Heaven, I murmur in English
after only one sip, but when I repeat it
in Spanish, Cielo thinks I've called her,
so she pushes her nose into my hand,
welcoming me even though service dogs
are only supposed to love
one person.

Herbivore

Ana

Leandro watches me devour
each delicious bite of everything
that was touched by his fingers
while he held the dough that created
these cookie hugs . . .

but las croquetas smell like ham
and las empanadas are picadillo, so I worry
about offending him if I refuse
to eat pork and beef.

In *The Book of Hope,* Jane Goodall tells a tale
about animals so intelligent and talented
that slaughtering them seems unimaginable.
There's a pig called Pigcasso, who loves
to dip his snout in paint, to make landscapes
so lovely that art collectors
regard them as treasures.

I try to apologize to Leandro,
but he shakes his head and grins.
Pigcasso? he murmurs, and at that moment
I know that when he borrowed my book,

he wasn't just trying to impress me.
He actually read about the artistic pig
and Jane Goodall's sources of hope—
nature's resilience, human resourcefulness,
the power of youth. . . .

She believes optimistic young people
can make the changes needed to heal Earth.
Eating less meat is just one way to reduce
our destructive impact.

Leandro takes my plate away
and quickly replaces it with one labeled
HERBIVORE, decorated with aromatic
green leaves—salvia, romero,
and laurel—along with edible flowers
that smell like
wilderness.

ABUNDANCE

Leandro

While I was reading about Pigcasso, I agreed
with Jane Goodall, and now I also empathize
with Ana, but each time I remember
my childhood hunger in Cuba,
waves of sorrow
overcome me.
I picture
the people
we left
behind:
primos
tías
abuelos,
all the relatives
who cannot join us
because the US has stopped
welcoming refugees.

Would my cousins, aunts, and grandparents
ever forgive me if I refused to cook and serve
this abundance to anyone who's hungry?

HIGH ABOVE THE ORDINARY WORLD
Ana

We sneak away
climb steep stairs
perch on a rooftop terrace
listen to the ocean's rhythmic whoosh,
Cielo's lighthearted hum, and our own
hushed voices
as we ask each other
if anyone else can see
this exhilarating gleam
when we touch.

Our first little kisses
are twinkles of brightness
on cheeks
foreheads
fingers
then
finally
lips
brushed
with lightning.

EYESHINE
Leandro

Some questions can't be answered
simply because the words don't exist yet.
I wish I knew how to invent an entirely new
vocabulary of descriptions for luminous
moments
like this.

I face Ana.
Her gaze meets mine.
We're human, so our eyes have no tapetum lucidum,
a reflective, iridescent layer behind the iris of animals,
allowing them to see in the dark and creating eyeshine—
blue for dogs, green for cats, white for tigers,
red for foxes, yellow for pumas.

Ana and I have only our true eye colors.
No iridescence, just natural emotions.
Is it too soon to tell her that she
makes me feel
incandescent?

HANDSHINE

Ana

he kisses
my fingers
then the palm
of my hand
the sheen
of touch
flows
from
lips
to lifeline.

THE DANCE CURE
Leandro

Overlooking the ocean
from this rooftop
with Ana in my arms
and Cielo at our side
I'm not terrified—waves
                    can't reach me,
depths won't drown us;
music flows up from below,
where other people are dancing
in their own sociable crowd,
while we're up here on our own,
wrapping each other
in clear air
and starlight.

Cielo the singing dog

in all my years
guarding the boy
and guiding him
I've never felt
more fearful

he's found
his scent match
but he has no way
to know that goals
are just the beginning
of long
complicated
journeys

The Morning after a First Kiss

Ana

Everything still feels magical.
At home on my sunporch
I read *The Plant Messiah*
by Carlos Magdalena
about rescuing
the last wild seeds
of endangered species
all over the world
to propagate them
at Kew Gardens in England,
then rewild the hopeful seedlings
back to their native habitats,
restoring biodiversity
for the green future.

Halfway through each page,
my mind drifts back to fingers, mouth,
eyes, and rooftop view, music floating up
from the patio below and from the song
of an unusual dog who reminds me that we all
hold treasures in our voices.

Sleepfulness

Ana

In the wild park
on my car-bed,
the unknown future
was so terrifying
that I chose
wakefulness
instead of
nightmares.

Now insomnia seems unimaginable.
All I want is more dreamtime
contigo
with you.

How strange it feels to wonder
if you're asleep too, soñando conmigo,
our daydreams fading into real ones
filled with iridescent
mindshine.

Beyond the Past
Ana

Other boys don't matter anymore,
all the crushes I thought of as almost-love
or nearly-there.

None of those eyes or hands
made me feel illuminated
and seen.

Other smiles were never like sunrise.
Other dances weren't enchanted portals.

I don't know what I'll do if you don't call
or text or show up at my door
ready
to kiss
and glow.

PATIENCE
Leandro

The bakery has swiftly grown popular
and crowded, with orders for birthday
and wedding cakes, catering, parties,
and so many cubano sandwiches
that my fingers ache from slicing bread,
and free time becomes a daydream,
abrazos are just cookies again, and there's no way
to see Ana outside of school hours, unless
I invite her on night hikes
in puma territory
just like the first time
our fingers
became lanterns . . .

but baking means waking up so early
that all I can manage is phone calls
with promises that feel
more like wishes.

Cielo the singing dog

aroma path waiting
my humans too busy

too busy for love
is always
a curse

TRADING LIFE STORIES
Ana

Late at night
far apart
we tell each other how much we love
nature, books, dogs, the wild park,
and the science
of hope.

It's such a relief
to hear and be heard
as our friendship
grows closer
even though all we have
is separate voices that travel across
the space   between   phones.

LEANDER AND HERO

Leandro

In world literature class
the teacher assigns an ancient Greek legend
about a youth with my name, and I learn
that "Leandro" means "lion-man."

He falls in love with a girl
who lives in a tower
by the sea.

Every night
she lights a torch so he can swim
across a strip of water like the one between Cuba
and Florida, so they can be together
for just a few
hours.

One evening a storm arises
the fierce wind blows out her torch's flame
and he loses his way
flails in the wrong direction
drowns, then washes ashore
near
the tower.

Hero dives
from the height
of her isolation
so she can join Leandro
in a lovers' tomb.

If I were the guy in this story
I could never drown
because I would not dare
to swim.

For Ana
would I
        try?

Habitat

Ana

I detest the story about Hero.
It's a tragedy, and I've already seen enough
suffering, just watching Mom mourn
the loss of Dad.

My life is still too uncertain.
All I crave
is hope.

It's a science with four skills for me to study.
Goals.
Pathways.
Confidence.
Support.

So I start with the first part.
I ask Leandro if he wants to start
a rewilding club at school.
Cielo can be a conservation dog again
for whatever project the club chooses—
helping an endangered species of plant
or animal, mapping populations
or rescuing surviving specimens,

locating whatever remnant of wilderness
professional biologists need to study.

We can ask our biology teacher to be the adviser.
Ms. Galán is AfroBoricua from Puerto Rico.
She has experience rescuing endangered parrots
after hurricanes, and she did her graduate work
in Portugal and Spain, helping to save
wolves and lynxes
by encouraging farmers
to protect their livestock
with guard dogs
instead of guns.

HOPE IS A SCIENCE

Leandro

If our goal is rewilding
and the pathway is a team,
then our teacher is support
and now all we need
is confidence.

ONE PERSON CAN RESCUE A SPECIES

Ana

Neiva Guedes saved blue macaws in Brazil.
Phyllis Ellman protected Tiburon mariposa lilies
in Marin County, and Ben Nyberg used drones
to locate the last three trees
of *Hibiscadelphus woodii*
on a cliff in Kauai.

Teamwork is even better—peregrine falcons,
California condors, sea otters, fen orchids,
blue whales, and golden lion tamarins
were all saved from extinction
by groups of scientists
working together
with volunteers . . .

but I can't stand the term "citizen scientist"
because it sounds like it's designed
to exclude new immigrants.

Wouldn't "community scientist"
be more inclusive?

COMMUNITY
Ana

The group that gathers for our first
rewilding club meeting is diverse
in so many ways—every skin color
and gender—all of us busy memorizing
one another's names and pronouns.

New friendships
seem possible.

Camila.
Tania.
Raidel.
Wave.
Yes, that last one is real, a name chosen
by his parents, who rode swells at Mavericks
when they were young and who now
volunteer with Leno, offering surf camps
to disabled children, to help them
feel safe in the water.

TEAMWORK
Leandro

Ms. Galán's land acknowledgment
to the Ohlone Nation
makes me feel
hypocritical.

If we know
it's their homeland,
why don't we
give it
back?

Instead, we plant silver lupines as a host
for the caterpillars of endangered
Mission blue butterflies,
and we clean trash
out of tide pools
at a marine preserve
where nocturnal harbor seals
reclaim the whole beach at exactly
10:00 a.m., flapping their flippers
against the surface of the ocean
to let us know that it's their turn
to stretch out in the sun
and sleep.

I shove all my anxieties about waves
and danger aside, making up my mind to ask
if there's a conservation dog project
I can join with Cielo.

Ms. Galán promises to introduce me to canines
and their handlers after I tell her about the panthers
in Florida, where Cielo's skills helped map the future
of wildlife crossings for saving a species.

It was a scientific experience
but magical, too,
just like Ana's
light.

EARLY SATURDAY MORNING
Leandro

Cielo and I stand in front of the cottage
at the nursery, while I wonder if I should have waited
until later—customers are already shopping for plants,
then wandering uphill toward a neighbor's field,
where Tío Leno is loading a giant pumpkin
onto a forklift for a contest in town
Monday morning, when las calabazas
will be weighed and chopped up
to make pies for the community food bank.

I should help my uncle, and Ana is probably
expected to sell trees and flowers with her mother
before we head out with the rewilding club
to plant blue violets as a host
for Oregon silverspot caterpillars,
but first we need to talk
and touch.

I'm desperate to know if we'll always be
luminous.

HUNGER

Ana

I'm peering into my phone
when I hear Cielo's song
as Leandro rings the front doorbell,
where there's a camera that records videos.
Last night it showed me
the face of a skinny puma prowling close
as she hunted during the dark hours,
gobbling a gopher, instead of the deer
she needs
for survival.

I open the door and pull Leandro into my arms
with Cielo pressed up against our legs, her nose
twitching as she sniffs the remnant odor
of a wildcat's hunger.

I'm hungry too.
I want more of those abrazos,
the sweet dulce de leche cookies,
and these hugs, the real ones made of arms
and radiance.

EMBRACE

Leandro

Ana shows me the screen of her phone.
A video of a lean, golden-eyed puma
capturing a rodent in front of the cottage
during the night.
The sounds
are eerie
chirps, a whistle,
no growl, just birdlike pleas
as if begging for meat.

Everything improbable is real now.
Ana's fingers on mine spark and shimmer.
We're like shape-shifters transformed
into candles.

With our arms around each other,
we might flare up and ignite.
What does it mean?
Am I dreaming?
I've never heard of anyone
who could set another person ablaze.

Only Cielo

Ana

We spend the whole morning outdoors
hands in soil, occasionally touching
just to see if anyone
notices.

No one
in the rewilding club
comments.

Leandro and I seem to be
wandering inside a fairy tale
with only a brilliant dog
to witness our secret.

Cielo the singing dog

scent is intelligence
the ability to identify
footprints
and other
love-lit
trails of
attachment

COLLEGE DREAMS
Leandro

Ms. Galán introduces me to Dr. Arturo Portuguéz Flores,
a retired professor from Mexico, who insists that I simply
call him Art, because he says we're equals,
one at the end
and one at the start
of wildlife biology careers.

He shows me how to monitor trail cameras
located near scrapes, which are places where pumas
stop to scratch the soil and deposit scent
announcing their availability as mates.

SAT prep, AP classes, application forms, an essay,
it's all stuff I've ignored until now, but with one more
whole year of high school still ahead of me,
maybe I can try.

Art says the University of Washington
has an excellent conservation dog program.

College Wishes

Ana

I love biology, but land use planning matters too.
I long to help figure out ways to create a balance
between rewilded green space
and homes for unhoused families.

Rent control?
Tiny homes?
Subsidies?
Charities?
I don't know where to start,
but that's the purpose of college, isn't it—
scientific and imaginative exploration?

Every Night

Ana

The female puma strolls
past a wooden bench in front of the cottage,
leaving a doorbell video for me to study
the next morning, watching
as she grows leaner,
half-starved
in need
of deer . . .

but the only time I see her dragging
the carcass of a fawn, she abandons it
as soon as the sound of Mom's alarm clock
startles her.

There are does and bucks who pass
through the nursery, but every time the puma
gets close, they flee to busy streets, where traffic
frightens the predator.

WILDLIFE CROSSINGS
Ana and Leandro

We study on our own at the library
so we'll know the right questions to ask
whenever we have a chance to spend time
with Art and the other puma project volunteers
who've welcomed our high school rewilding club
into their wildlife rescue work.

California's mountain lions are divided
into ten separate populations, genetic islands
separated by highways, where fast cars
prevent males from ranging far enough
to find mates who aren't closely related.

Inbreeding has already resulted in mutations,
both nonlethal ones like twisted tails
and deadly ones
emerging from
defective sperm.

The world's largest wildlife crossing
is scheduled to start construction on Earth Day
near Los Angeles, but we need them up here
in the San Francisco Bay Area, too, so pumas

east of Silicon Valley can reach the ones
in beach towns.

Wildlife detection dogs are already at work,
searching for ideal locations
that follow a trail
of scrapes.

PRETENDING

Leandro

While I wait to find out
if the conservation dog team
will accept me and Cielo
even though I'm not quite
eighteen yet, it's easy to relax
and imagine success.

I used to know how to swim and surf
before the tragedy of the raft.

I used to ask for whatever I needed
when I was small and talkative.

Then Papi drowned
and I stopped speaking
to strangers
like that teacher
who revealed
my family's
dangerous
secret . . .

but that was then and this is now.

I need free time, less work, more study,
and more, more, more Ana, so I ask Tío Leno
to hire a real baker, and soon he's replaced me
with two full-time experts, so I only have to make
cakes and cookies, empanadas y pastelitos
y frituras
y croquetas
once in a while,
when the bakery is super busy
and Ana can come with me
to taste samples before they vanish.

Without thinking about waves,
the first thing I ask her to do
when I have a truly free day
is take Cielo to the beach
to watch the sunset
and pretend
I'm brave.

Will I Be Fearful Forever?

Leandro

Emilio is in community college,
where he's joined a surfing team that competes.
They often win, but when they're not traveling,
they volunteer to teach surf camps
for disabled children, who climb
onto sturdy boards
and face small swells
that threaten to trigger
my panic.

How can such young kids be courageous
while I'm such a coward?

So I dare myself
to join them.

Ana is so confident in the water
that she splashes and dives under waves,
then helps a blind girl who listens
to Cielo's humming
and my brother's instructions—relax
enjoy
inhale

balance
imagine
be patient
believe.

But belief
isn't enough.

My mind
is not in control.

Fear
is a tyranny that rules
inside my heart.

You Could Try

Ana

Just when we've reached all sorts of unspoken
understandings, I make the mistake
of saying words that horrify Leandro—try
wading
just up to your knees.

Oh, what a disaster, and it's all
my fault. I should have kept
my mouth shut. Why didn't I
believe his description
of overwhelming

                    panic?

I'm the same way on airplanes
because I'm afraid of my father,
the rage-filled pilot.

I should have imagined that fear of a person
could be transferred
to water.

WHEN I TRY
Leandro

My lungs
forget
      how to breathe

mind can't manage
           to believe

all I do is remember
how I was swept off a raft
by the immense wave
that made
Papi
           need to save me
by leaping off
tossing me back up
and then losing his own   struggle
to reach
climb
grasp
cling.

SEPARATE

Ana

Leandro won't look at me. He just
holds on to Cielo.
I would breathe
for him if I could, but he's
already seated on
rough sand, defeated
and slumped
as if dreaming,
all trace of
closeness
to real
life
lost.

DIM
Leandro

We try to fly back to that moment
right before I time traveled onto
                        the raft,

but there's no way to recapture
                        free air.

When Ana talks to me, I only hear
                        echoes
                    of her voice.
My own mind is
                    trapped
                            far away

        beneath

        waves.

Have You Tried . . .

Ana   *Leandro*

medicine   of course
counseling   por supuesto
group therapy   yes
visualization
mindfulness
meditation
ice on the back
of the neck
to help you
relax

                  sí, sí, sí

        now
    when our fingers
intertwine
                the light is purple
a bruise
        not a shine

CAMOUFLAGE

Leandro

For three years after Papi drowned,
Mami only wore black, then for the next three years,
black and white, and now she dresses like a female bird
in nesting season, subtle gray or dull brown, each feather
streaked with
memory.

Instead of the clothing of mourning,
something in my childhood's small self
chose a cloak of dry land, each footstep
ghostly.

So I stay on dry land with Cielo,
wishing I understood
freedom.

DOWNPOUR

Ana

Exactly one week before Halloween,
while we're still in the midst of our own gloom,
a climate catastrophe sweeps
all other emotions
                              away.
Only the weather forecast matters today.
Atmospheric river
                    bomb cyclone
          tornado-like
                    spiral
                         of
                         wind
caused by a sudden drop
               in pressure, and then
the rain stalls, canyons are flooded,
tent cities
                         plunge,
landslides roll and tumble until
                         unhoused people are buried
                         under   mud.

Refugees Need Food

Leandro   *Ana*

The high school becomes an evacuation center.
The bakery turns into a community food bank.

Papi's bread recipe   crusty outside.
keeps my hands busy   soft inside.
fragrant dough   blazing oven
knife   slice
fill   offer
sandwiches   free
        served with cookie abrazos,
    edible hugs for frightened children.

FRIENDS NEED FOOD

Ana

Tania and Raidel from the rewilding club
are two of the people who thank us
for sandwiches y abrazos.

Until this moment I had no idea that they
are unhoused and that Tania despises the term,
insisting—just as I used to—that it's a euphemism,
not a solution to the real problem
of homelessness
due to high prices
gentrification
Silicon Valley's
greed.

DAREDEVIL
Ana

Leandro is still busy making sandwiches
when rescue swimmers from the fire department
are called out to Mavericks, the monstrous waves
off-shore, enormous swells that rise as high
as three-story buildings
whenever there's a storm.

I'm at the high school with Tania and Raidel,
handing out sandwiches, juice, and cookies
when the news comes that Emilio is among
a handful of surfers who ignored warnings
to stay out of the dangerous ocean.

Leno is furious
and worried. He rushes
to the hospital, calls Dulce
and Leandro, then Mom, so that soon
we're all in a waiting room
expecting the worst.

VIGIL

Leandro

Hard chairs.
Dull walls.
Muted voices.
Slow clock.

Maddening
need for patience.

Cielo tries to soothe me
with her softly humming
dog voice.

Ana holds my hand
even though our skin
barely
shimmers
just
a
flicker
of sorrowful
darkness.

Survivors
Leandro

Even with his heaviest wet suit,
Emilio stayed under turbulent currents for so long
that his temperature plunged below 82 degrees,
the threshold between moderate and severe
hypothermia, a deadly condition—lethargy
progressing to organ failure.

Nearly comatose in a hospital bed,
he hardly resembles the muscular athlete
we're all so accustomed to worrying about
whenever waves are ferocious enough to attract
his excitement.

How did one brother grow so fearless
and the other so profoundly terrified
on that day when our father was swallowed
by the sea?

By the time Emilio opens his eyes,
I'm already lost in the fear

                                    of loss.

Near Panic

Ana

This time
you don't fall
because Cielo recognizes the odor
of fight-or-flight chemicals, adrenaline,
and all your other invisible clues
to a racing heart
and strangled breath.

You sit quietly,
obeying your intuitive dog,
my hand still wrapped
around yours even though
I'm not sure you're aware
that we're once again
a fountain
of flowing
light.

Cielo the singing dog

watch me
match my rhythm

touch me
catch this melody

follow me
along the song-trail that leads
to survival

I remember the raft too
but there were ancestors dancing
all around us
then
and here they are
now
again
      again
           again

SUSTO

Leandro

The first time I fainted from a panic attack
was in Miami, soon after the raft, while watching
a weather forecast on the news, with storm waves
that seemed like living monsters once again
swallowing Papi.

Mami took me to a curandera,
who diagnosed susto, a uniquely Cuban malady
caused by fright.

My skin was cleansed with aromatic leaves,
incantations, and a whole egg that was used
like a broom, the bone-hued shell brushing my skin
until I was expected to feel new.

The limpia worked, but not for long.
My mind kept tumbling back into the ocean
sunken
suffocated
submerged.

Beginner's Mind
Leandro

A middle school counselor once taught me
how to breathe deeply, depending on Cielo
to calm my fears with childlike wonder,
a practice he called beginner's mind,
as if I'm a newborn baby seeing
shapes and colors
for the first time.

Whenever I manage to remember
how to feel like an infant, waves become
just one of many natural marvels
monstrous only at midnight
in sinking
                    dreams,
and then at dawn
the memory of an eggshell
returns,
helping me feel
renewed.

IMAGINARY JOURNEY

Leandro

My daredevil brother is safe now.
I fall asleep in a chair, and in my brain's
dreaming eye, I see how Ana and I float
together, at the center of a moonlit lake
calm water
no waves
but so cold
and immense
that I know
I can never reach shore unless I try,
so I learn how to swim again, and by the end
of that dream-night
we're on land
in sunlight
resting
warm.

Watching You
Ana

When you gave sandwiches
to homeless people during that storm
you were the most heroic being
I've ever seen.

Then you sat here with your brother
even though you were furious with him
for being so reckless and selfish—he's an adult,
a community college student.
He should know better than to make
your mother suffer.

Men who think they have to be tough
are wrong.

Kindness.
That's what you are,
all I need, a different way
of being strong.

MICRO-JOY
Leandro

After panic
and turmoil,
after worry
and near loss,
I treasure
every small
beauty
tiny
pleasures
outdoor
clear air
breath
scent
sight
light
sky
mind
luminous.

ONE MARACA

Ana

tonight
all I need is one
rhythmic gourd rattle
and a flick of my wrist
to connect me deeply
with centuries
I'll never see
sound
songs
words
verse
sand
shakes
time's
dance

HALLOWEEN

Leandro

Emilio has recovered.
Leno forgives him.
Mami is silent.

Ana and I are close again,
gleaming beneath eerie green
makeup, wigs, and costumes
that transform us into
human-shaped trees,
our hair leafy
hands bright
hearts
flowering
with gifts
of candy
for children.

DAY OF THE DEAD

Ana   Leandro

El Día de los Muertos
is not a popular holiday in Cuba,
where no one goes to the cemetery
unless they have died or to bury a loved one,
but we decide to build an altar in the bakery
                    for Papi

with ofrendas

                    of candles
wildflowers

                    fresh bread
herbs

                    and little poems that sound
                    like maracas
and dancers   because

        no one is ever
    alone in a graveyard's
          embrace
        surrounded
       by ancestors.

ROLE MODELS
Ana

In biology class we take turns naming
people who inspire us.

Leandro talks about his papi's admiration
for Chef José Andrés, who always feeds everyone
during any natural or man-made disaster.

I choose George Meléndez Wright,
the first scientifically trained wildlife biologist
ever hired to lead the National Park Service.
He convinced Congress to stop letting rangers
kill predators, so in my opinion he was
the first rewilder, even though plenty
of other lighter-skinned people
have received the credit.

As a group, the rewilding club chooses
Jane Goodall, for teaching us that hope
is a science.

DNA

Leandro

Art and Ms. Galán help us collect puma hair
in a snare made of tangled branches, so we
can send it to a lab for analysis.

The big male in the wild park
and the lean female at the nursery
are not closely related.

They can mate safely,
but busy highways separate them,
so traffic is the biggest obstacle
to the creation of the next generation.

The only thing we can do is advocate
for the construction of a wildlife crossing
that would cost millions of dollars.

Every evening I kiss Ana at the sunroom door
and then wait for her to show me a video
the next morning, after nightmares
followed by dawn.

CAONA

Ana

Most pumas are labeled with numbers
like P-22 in Los Angeles, who is famous
for posing near the Hollywood sign
and for hunting a koala at the zoo
and for being unable to mate
because there's no way he can cross
so many busy freeways to reach
the wild mountains.

I don't want a number or tracking collar
for the female who shows up in front of the cottage
over and over, as if she expects me
to invite her in, so I name her secretly,
knowing I'm being unscientific.

"Caona" means "gold" in Taíno.
It's the color of her eyeshine
and my wishes.

DILEMMA

Ana

Pumas aren't called big cats
because they can't roar like tigers,
lions, or leopards, but they do purr,
and their babies are often called kittens
even by scientists.

One morning in mid-November, I peer
at the doorbell video and realize
that despite her visible ribs,
Caona's belly is sagging—she's pregnant,
and with only a ninety-day gestation,
she'll give birth close to Valentine's Day.

There's no way to help her hunt deer,
so I'm tempted to feed her. Then she won't
have to keep eating rodents, which might carry
the danger of rat-killing poisons, anticoagulants
used by gardeners and farmers
even though they're deadly
to the entire natural
food chain.

Cielo the singing dog

the scent of future events
would be soothing
if our world
were still ancient
so that wildness
could win

I Ask Myself Questions

Ana

Watching Caona's hunger
is painful, and keeping the videos
to myself would feel dishonest,
so I show each one
to Leandro,
and he
shares them
with wildlife biologists,
while I keep asking myself
whether I should feed a few steaks
to the suffering cat, or just wait and see
if she manages to survive.

The experts say female pumas catch deer
but abandon them too easily whenever they hear
human voices or the roar of a car, while males
tend to stay and defend a carcass, confident
that they can defeat scavengers.

Is it wrong to want to help a wild animal
who seems like she needs friendship?

WEAKNESS
Leandro

The videos are disturbing.
A pregnant puma, half-starved.

There must be some reason
for her ordeal—was she an orphan
whose mother never had a chance
to teach her how to hunt?

Maybe she's sick.
Pumas catch feline viruses from house cats,
and they get poisoned by eating squirrels
that have consumed rodenticides.

Art says we won't know unless she's sedated
and examined by veterinarians, but tranquilizers
could be dangerous for the unborn kittens.

It's a decision for scientists,
not high school kids.

THANKSGIVING IS A DAY
OF MOURNING

Ana

I can't cook at all, and Mom isn't much better,
so we eat at the bakery, a herbivore's feast
of frijoles negros, arroz con azafrán, yuca, malanga,
plátanos maduros, and a dessert called tocino del cielo—
bacon of heaven, which is really just a tricky name
for an egg-rich custard the color and sheen
of translucent amber that reminds me
of Caona's eyeshine.

Thanksgiving is a day of mourning
for many indigenous communities,
but I feel grateful for Mom, Leandro,
his family, and our rewilding club friends,
as well as Ms. Galán and Art, who join us
for the meal and lead the way in making
a land acknowledgment
to the Ohlone Nation.

Thanksgiving Is a Day
for Actions of Gratitude
Leandro

El día de acción de gracias
is a day for taking action, so we roast a piglet,
bake bread, and make so many sandwiches
that it takes all of us to carry them
to the families who live
in tents
on stream banks
all over the coast.

Tania and Raidel help
because they understand
better than anyone
just how hungry
the children are
in homeless camps.

Stalker

Ana

Home.
Silence.
Midnight
insomnia
from excitement
and drinking too much
café cubano, along with
the satisfaction of taking food
to unhoused families.

A chime.
The doorbell camera
announces the arrival of a creature
large enough to set off the motion detector.

So I watch
from the safety of bed,
but what I see is not the usual
prowling puma, with her pregnant belly
and glowing
golden eyes.
This time it's Dad
peering in through our front window
like a burglar.

He stares
as if he can see me,
then grins at the camera
in a weird way,
his face and hands tattooed
with ominous designs
that make him look
ferocious.

Are they violent
militia
symbols?

He doesn't knock,
and I don't go to the door.

Instead, I hide on the sunporch,
where I convince myself that by morning
his presence will turn out to be nothing more
than a nightmare or my imagination. . . .

EMERGENCY

Ana

It wasn't a dream.
My father was here.

Mom saw the video too.
The police measured his shoe prints,
and now they're warning us to stay
somewhere else for a few days, but first
we have to talk to the FBI, answering a strange series
of creepy questions
that makes me feel unreal.

Dad's list of crimes has grown dramatically.
Weapons of war, bombs, stolen drones,
and money, millions, so much theft
and fraud. . . .

We have to leave.
He's the fugitive,
but somehow
we're the ones
forced to hide.

EXILE

Ana

I can't even tell Leandro where we'll be
because Mom seizes my phone and laptop
while she orders me
to be patient.

On the Pacific Coast Highway,
we flee secretively, like refugees.
One hour passes and then another
until we're parking behind a lighthouse
somewhere in Santa Cruz County,
our car hidden
by tumbled rocks
and drifting fog.

Isolation.
Secrecy.
I might as well be unhoused again
or lost in time on some distant shore
with only sea lions and otters
as witnesses.

You Vanish Like a Shadow
Leandro

Heart
knotted
hands
empty
the landscape
of my thoughts
narrowed
un ciclón
a storm
inside
my bones
all the fiery
meteors
between us
where?

Cielo the singing dog

instinct
is my true leash

I could find her if only my nose
were set free to inhale the aerial
movements
of grief

LIFE IN A LIGHTHOUSE
Ana

Spiral
   staircase
view
  of sea mist
aroma
     of salt
sorrow's
        height
sunlight's
       absence
so why
      does
this tower
        feel
like
the
deepest
burial?

DISBELIEF
Leandro

No call, text, video,
or handwritten oak-gall-ink
love note.

I'm almost too angry for sadness.
Everyone says don't worry; there must be
some explanation . . .

but I don't believe them,
especially not Tío Leno.
I'm sure my uncle must know something,
but he won't betray Rosa's need for secrecy,
not even when it means that he's leaving me
helpless.

So much for thinking of hope as a science.
It's more like an archaic form of torture.

THE GEOGRAPHY OF A LIGHTHOUSE

Ana

Downstairs there are beds, food, a table,
and books, but no phone or TV, no radio,
not even an old-fashioned magazine
or newspaper.

Mom sleeps a lot.
I dance alone.

Each night I climb the spiral staircase
to a round room with huge windows
and a lifeless lamp, a broken artifact
from some long-lost era when ships
had nothing but a giant light bulb
for guidance.

How long do we have to stay here?
            Will I ever hold you again?
                        Will we glow?

In every direction all I see is ravenous fog
                        swallowing all the stars.

Immensity

Ana

This ocean is called Pacific,
but it's never peaceful.

Endless waves crash against rocks,
then roll away like an army of dragons
fuming with rage.

Risk

Ana

I swim alone while Mom sleeps
even though I know it's dangerous.

What else can I do on this shore
with only mist and sea-foam
for companionship?

I thought I believed in free will and destiny
at the same time, but now I wonder if we
were just a fantasy, luminous and fleeting,
so I hold my breath
plunge
swirl
away
from
my
own
mind.

I KEEP WONDERING
Ana

What's next?
No school
or career?

An eternity
of fear?

No love
or light?

Only this
half-alive
ocean
of wishes?

NUMB

Ana

I can't cry,
but I scream
until Mom finally
talks to me.

She admits that Leno
arranged this hiding place
and the FBI agreed
on the condition
that no one else knows,
not even you, Leandro,
so I'm guessing you assume
that I'm really gone
instead of just
phoneless
and silent.

I Miss You

Leandro

Leno promises me that you're safe,
but without hearing your voice
or touching your light,
all I wonder is what
would happen if I tried to find you
the old way, by tying a black cloth to a chair
or turning a statue of a saint upside down
or piercing your footprint with a sharply
carved stick, but there's no folkloric
tracking cure
for locating someone
hidden by law enforcement.

Leno told me about your father,
so I know you're hiding, and all my mind craves
is your safety, but my heart wants you here
close to my own
confusion.

Cielo the singing dog

he hears when I hum
natural rhythms to slow
his heart's drum.

GLIMPSES
Leandro

I start seeing the lean puma everywhere,
late at night on the patio of the bakery
and in bright daylight, near the beach
or running across roads and parking lots,
sending strangers
into a frenzy
of dangerous
wildlife
selfies.

Each time I see her golden eyeshine
beneath streetlights
I make a call to Art,
who helps me file an official incident report
with the California Department of Fish and Wildlife.

They decide not to move her.
It would require shooting her
with a tranquilizer dart, a trauma
too risky while she's pregnant.

TERRITORIAL
Leandro

Art insists that even if they moved the puma
and fitted her with a tracking collar,
she would probably soon return.

Cats are like homing pigeons,
always seeking the safety
of a familiar den.

Sometimes I feel like you
are my only true home, Ana Tanamá,
and any mountain or shore will be easy
to love, as long as we keep our hands
intertwined
pools
of brightness
shining between
our fingers.

DOG-JOY
Leandro

Scared and restless, I try to wait patiently,
but it's better to hike, camp, and swim
in a quiet lake, my only way to prove
that I'm brave.

Still water never frightens me,
and tracking puma scrapes feels safe.
Hardly anyone ever gets killed
by predators in California.
We live in a land where cars
are the greatest danger.

I'm pretty sure my dog understands
because her dilated nostrils keep leading me
from one fierce aroma to another
as if I'm half canine
with a mindful
nose.

CHRISTMAS EVE

Ana

silhouettes of birds pass
beyond the lighthouse windows
wings in slow motion

wind swirls dense fog
while I imagine my future—
endless solitude

CHRISTMAS DAY
Leandro

Ordinarily I would make
buñuelos de yuca drizzled with anise syrup,
and five varieties of turrón nougat candy,
and sweet corn tamales wrapped in green
banana leaves, and deep-fried chiviricos
sprinkled with sugar.

This year I don't cook anything.
With Cielo at my side, I help Art
check all the trail cameras in parks
and one we've added near the nursery,
where everything is locked up, all the workers
are on vacation, and a sign on the gate
states CLOSED, without any indication
of a normal future.

I Fill My Imagination with Words

Ana

"querer"
means "to want"

"amar"
is "to love"

sometimes
they're the same
or maybe a little bit
different

"esperar"
means "wait"

but "esperanza"
is "hope"

and the Taíno word for "beginning"
is "bi"
all I want is

a chance to start over. . . .

NEW YEAR'S EVE
Ana

no kiss
just wishes
imagination
my only
future

THREE KINGS DAY
Leandro

On El Día de los Tres Reyes Magos
I decide to create a book-filled gift
so it will be waiting for Ana
whenever she returns.

Heart-shaped knots
decorate the carved pine boards
that I stain with an oak hue
to make a Little Free Library
in front of the locked-up nursery,
where only a hungry puma
and my silent daydreams
ever visit.

I fill the shelves with poetry, science,
and stories, and then I add *The Book of Joy*,
a collection of conversations between
the Dalai Lama and Archbishop Desmond Tutu,
both of them old men who remained youthful
by telling jokes, teasing, even dancing
just for the sheer fun of movement.

THE SECOND-WORST DAY OF MY LIFE

Ana

Three Kings Day marks exactly one year
since I watched violence on the news
as extremists tried to overthrow
the elected US government.

Dad was on TV.
I saw his scowl.
I watched him smash
a metal bar into the face
of a policewoman.

That's when I gave up hoping
that my parents would ever
get back together.

I thought it would always be my worst sorrow
until the day Mom brought me here,
making me hide so far away from you
that everything feels like endings,
nothing ever
starting over.

SCHOOL WITHOUT YOU
Leandro

I don't even try to listen.
Nothing makes any sense.
Teachers sound pompous.
Friends are annoying.
I won't answer all these nosy questions
about where you've gone, are you sick,
did we break up, am I going to join
the next rewilding club field trip,
did I hear about the puma
who ran into an office building
in Irvine, or the one found inside
a high school English classroom
in Pescadero, and what about
the shark attack at Lover's Point
and junior prom
will I still go
without you?

I Imagine You
Ana

as I swim

far

beyond

rough boulders

I dare

this furious ocean

to defeat me with its power

when I'm already

almost completely

lost

FINALLY!

Leandro

Tío Leno says the emergency is over!
¡Se acabó!
No more need for you to hide.
No more threat from your greedy dad.
You and Rosa can return
to your cottage at the nursery,
where you and I can figure out how
to start over as if you'd never
disappeared.

When Leno invites me to go with him
to bring you back, Cielo leaps into the van
as if she knows where we're going and why.
Dogs are so much smarter than anyone
realizes, especially in this wordless realm
of roaring, howling
emotions!

SCINTILLATION
Ana

The melody of Cielo's voice
reaches my ears
      above water's percussion
as I push away fear
and spontaneously dive
swimming
underwater
toward shore

then above   bodysurfing
each wave's   force   brings me closer
         to you   until
finally
¡al fin!
       hands
    hair
  lips
 tangled
limbs
ablaze!

INCOMPREHENSIBLE
Leandro

I don't know
how the fear of losing you
became greater than the fear
of water

I can't stop to figure out why
panic did not keep me from
diving
toward
you

or why
I didn't faint

or whether I can ever
be brave again

all I know is that we
are together
safe
now
this
light.

You Threw Yourself into the Sea for Me!

Ana

Panic
is as unpredictable
as rogue waves.

How
did
you
dive?

Where
was
your
fear?

Why are we able to set ourselves ablaze
even in water
churning?

BLAZE

Leandro   *Ana*

cold   soaked
flare   pulse
you   us
air   salt
shore   tears
shiver   bright
sun   warmth
              alive
              alive
              alive

Cielo the singing dog

relief
      ablaze
            love
                soars
                  above
                    love

SHORE

Ana

fog
mist
wind
cold beyond cold
folds over us
fingers lace together
we form a net to catch
and hold
flashes
of
sun
this
warmth
awake
awake
awake

LOOK
Leandro

There was a day in world literature class
when the teacher told us that the sculptor Rodin
once told the poet Rilke
to go to the zoo
and *look*
at a panther.

The verse that resulted was bittersweet
with captive muscles and wild feline eyes,
and while he was there Rilke also wrote
his famous poem about a graceful swan.

Now, as we walk into the lighthouse
salty, sandy, wet, and shivering,
I *look*
at you
and see
that same
caged desperation
combined with feathery wings
this possibility of freedom.

EXTORTION

Ana

No one explains anything
until all four of us are safe
in the bakery the next morning,
guzzling café con leche and devouring
dulce de guayaba con queso.

Men who think other men should never cry
don't understand the sensitive strength
of Leandro and Leno; they're both
just as tearful as Mom and me.

Leno's story is so bizarre that I have to force myself
to listen to all the mystifying details, the ransom note
he received from my father in advance of any actual
kidnapping—it's the kind of protection money
demanded by mob bosses and by bandits
long ago, in the countryside of Cuba
during the chaos after Spain
was defeated, when the US
claimed the island
as a territory, trying
to prevent
independence.

Dad's ransom note specified cryptocurrency,
five million dollars, an underworld account number
with numbers that can't be traced . . .

but if Leno had paid,
then the criminal—Dad—would still be free,
while Mom and I would remain vulnerable,
so federal agents were informed, and the rest
sounds like bizarre scenes
from an old gangster movie.

Dad was arrested near the nursery,
still searching for us, wearing body armor
and carrying two assault rifles, even though
he knew we would not be prepared
to defend ourselves
against love that somehow
turned into hatred.

MYTHICAL

Ana

I don't know why,
but I need to imagine
that someday I might be able
to think of Dad as a person again
instead of a hybrid beast
like the Minotaur
or Cyclops.

Picturing him as an archetype
makes him seem too powerful
and permanent, while humans
are predictably
short-lived.

SING TO YOUR FOOD

Ana

I never met my abuelos,
but Mom told me her parents always sang
before they ate, a rhythm of gratitude
preceding fullness, la melodía
and all the words constantly changing
improvised halfway between the belly's joy
and a voice
from the heart.

It's the same for me now.
Having lived through danger
helps me appreciate each crumb,
each sip, each breath, all of it changing
from sunlight to green leaves
and then back again,
sparkling inside
my mind
a dance
of gratitude.

LIGHT BETWEEN SHADOWS
Leandro

we move through each day
dreamlike, two human splashes
of shimmering sun

A Home Called Tomorrow

Ana

Poetry and science
in the Little Free Library
offer themselves to me as if you
have transformed yourself
into paper, ink, time,
and daydreams.

The Book of Joy
makes me feel
limitless.

It's the sweetest gift,
but I can't figure out
what to offer you in return
after being away
for so many days
in such a strange way
as if I'd been hidden
on some remote planet
and now you've willed me
back to Earth.

THE PEACE OF WILD PLACES
Leandro

Ana's late Christmas gift for me is a Saturday drive
all the way north to the tallest coastal redwoods,
where each tree's size and age feels sacred.

Everything is ancient and alive!
The forest smells like growth and time.

Cielo roams with us, leading the way
from roots and needles on the ground
to air and sun in each other's eyes.

The whole world is a soothing place to rest
like the one in that Wendell Berry poem
about the peace of wild things.

So we lie down on a blanket and listen
to the bird calls
of each other's
heartbeats.

CAT IN A TREE

Ana

We arrive back at the nursery
exhausted and ravenous,
planning to cook, eat, and sing
to our food, but it's twilight,
and in one of the old oak trees
along the roadside
I spot Caona
perched
on a heavy branch
eyes glowing, mouth open in
a silent snarl, either fury or fear. . . .

I stay in the car with Cielo
while Leandro goes out to talk to the puma,
who seems to need some sort of reassurance
that she'll have a safe home of her own
someday.

CAUTION

Leandro

Talking to a puma sounds foolish
unless your entire life has been spent
in constant conversation with a dog
who answers in her own language
of movements and music, a wordless
vocabulary of instinct.

The cat gazes down from an oak branch.
All it would take for her to crack my neck open
is one swift
bite.

Pumas can leap fifteen feet straight up
or thirty feet ahead. They never roar, only snarl,
chirp like birds, or wail like ghosts. . . .

So I make myself tall as I reach up and sing
until she closes her eyes, leaving me free
to retreat to the car, where I show Ana
a photo of the cat's eye, a close-up,
the pupil round and black, surrounded
by gold, and rimmed
            with a rippled line

of darker copper
        an eye so intensely
predatory
        that I know
I've survived
        this encounter
only because
        I reached my arms high
and forced my voice
        to sound enormous.

RELIEF

Ana

I shouldn't have named a wild creature.
I can't pretend to understand anything
about nature, not until I learn how to listen
and observe like a true scientist.

I'm not even good at interpreting
the actions of people.

After leaving Caona perched in the oak,
I sit on the sunporch with Leandro, but I can't explain
how I feel about his bravery around wildlife
and the way he was able to leap into the ocean
and swim when he thought I was drowning
near the lighthouse.

He didn't panic until afterward,
when we were both safe.

Is the courage of love
a bridge
or a boat?

BRIDGES AND TUNNELS
Ana

I help you bake.
I'm learning to cook.
Together there's nothing
we can't accomplish
in a kitchen
or a library
or the wild park,
where we keep hiking
with Cielo, as she becomes
an expert at detecting puma trails.

With guidance from librarians at UC Berkeley,
we research the history of wildlife crossings.

The Trans-Canada Highway has forty bridges
and tunnels to help animals migrate
and find mates.

In Kenya there are underpasses for elephants,
in Singapore, bridges for pangolins, in Australia,
tunnels for penguins, and in Costa Rica, ropes
between trees so sloths and monkeys can travel
high above roads, even in places where the forest
has been logged.

Sometimes I feel
like you and I
are on a rope bridge
of our own
a swaying
braid
of strands
that we weave
as we walk
creating
our dizzy
aerial
pathway
of
hope

The Hardest Part is Still Ahead
Ana

I'll have to testify at Dad's trial
for seditious conspiracy to overthrow
the US government, attempted kidnapping
of his own daughter, and dozens of other
heartbreaking charges.

Dad the Minotaur, Dad the Cyclops,
my father the monster will see me in court
and know that I don't forgive him—not yet,
maybe never, even though Mom says she suspects
that he's been tricked by white supremacists
who managed to teach him how to hate himself
and us.

WORD ORIGINS

Ana

Mom will soon be divorced.
If she marries Leno,
he will be my stepfather.

What does that even mean—step?
It sounds like the first part of a very slow
journey from then
to now
and someday
when . . .

so I look in a dictionary
where I see that the origin of "step"
is from the German word "stoep."

It means "orphan"
just as "unhoused"
means "homeless."

TSUNAMI WARNING
Leandro

Just when everything feels almost a little bit
balanced
and steady, an alarm sounds on my phone
and every other
screen in town, alerting the whole community
to the danger
of a massive wave from the violent eruption
of a distant volcano
in the South Pacific, on Tonga, thousands
of miles away.

The tsunami is approaching
  California, Oregon, and Washington
    at a speed of five hundred miles per hour,
      traveling toward us like a meteor in space,
        bringing whitewater, a churn of height
          without any predictable shape that a surfer
            might safely ride, and the reef beneath Mavericks
              will make it even more risky, exactly the sort
                of impossible challenge
                  that my brother craves.

DIZZY

Leandro

Once again I find myself perched
on the bluffs above towering waves, waiting
to see if Emilio
will survive
                his effort to
                        tame
                chaotic
        oceanic
terror.

I shouldn't be here,
        but I have to at least try
                to be ready to help in some
                        unforeseen way
                                in case of
                                        disaster.

Cielo the singing dog

hum breathe
    sing touch
trust sit stay
    safe

Precipice

Ana

Everything looks impossible—
the massive size of unruly waves
and the courage of rogue surfers
and the generosity
of rescuers,
but how many times
can they save the same rule-breakers
without giving up
and just letting them paddle

                           farther and farther . . . ?

Beside me, you tremble
while your dog hums
softly.

I lunge just in time
to force you down from panic
onto cold ground, where you can't
       topple
     faint
  fall.

FAINTING
Leandro

panic
volcanic
turbulent
furious
awareness
words
confusing
words
mysterious
words
incomplete
sentences
of
hurt

I Drive You Home from the Edge of Disaster

Ana

Exhausted,
you need to rest,
so I help your mami and tío
slice bread for sandwiches
that we'll take to San Bruno,
where immigrants from Tonga
await news of their loved ones
in villages that might not exist
anymore, swept away by lava
or the tsunami.

Islanders
from every part of the world
understand the patience that's needed
to await tales of survival
whenever a peaceful sea
suddenly becomes
a mythical
creature.

TRANSLUCENT

Leandro

While I was lost in sleep-drenched darkness
my mind never imagined this glossy awakening
in daytime, as I float now, high above
past sorrows.

Your fingers almost touch my face
and the air between us
ignites.

I clasp your shimmering hand.
Light emerges and flows
right through me.

Peace
is so luminous
and short-lived.
Sooner or later
we'll return
to reality.

Together We Drift . . .

Ana

through minutes
and hours
of kisses

nothing matters
beyond this closeness

we share sunlight
between shadows

even in dense fog
we shine

love creates
its own floating
          brightness

MIDNIGHT ANXIETIES

Ana

Darkness refuses to let us rest.
We fall into our separate bouts of insomnia,
trying to escape the shared fear
of nightmares.

Your terrors are always wave-shaped,
while mine range from Dad's tattooed face
to the starvation of puma kittens whose mother
can't find enough food to fuel her flow of milk.

In every one of my heaviest worries,
I'm always houseless
just like
before.

SUCCESS FOLLOWS FAILURE
Leandro

Only my brother seems to know exactly
where he's going now, his sudden decision
to transform himself into a rescue swimmer,
one of the most perfect examples of human
metamorphosis
I've ever witnessed.

Trying to surf on tsunamis and storm waves
was so dangerous that he abruptly turned away
from near death and accepted a different vision
of his future.

He's a Fire Academy student now,
preparing for disasters.

He wants to be a hero,
not a victim.

JUNIOR PROM
Ana

Blue dress
  starlit
moon soothed
  spirit
dance mind
   drumlike
hearts
  entwined
your light
  and mine
rhythmic

PROM NIGHT EUPHORIA
Ana and Leandro and Cielo

girl, boy, dog
all singing together
a wilderness of melodies
this music a true joy
as if feral voices
might last
forever . . .

LATE-NIGHT SURPRISE
Leandro

I left the bakery van near the sunroom door
so we could go to prom together in Ana's car.

Now, after dancing and twirling as if we were birds,
we return to find the puma underneath the van,
perhaps absorbing whatever residual heat the engine
might still be releasing,
hopefully enough
to keep her warm
because she looks
so needy, emaciated,
and no longer
pregnant.

Where are the kittens?
Has she lost them or left them
in a secret den on some rocky slope,
and why does Ana insist on calling her Caona
when she knows we're not supposed to name
wild animals
as if they are pets?

Cielo the singing dog

I know the scent of birth
and afterbirth

I would follow the cat to her den
        if my service dog vest was off
            replaced by the harness
            and long leash I wear
                for tracking feline scat
                and tracks

but moonlight
roots us in place all night
as we watch
wait
inhale
this wild stench
of hunger

PUMA BLUES

Ana

Euphoria
fades to worry.

Anxiety
replaces joy.

We watch from the sunporch doorway,
wondering whether any of Caona's kittens
survived.

Cielo lifts her nose to inhale a plume of air.
Can a dog detect the future just by breathing
a fragrance of safety?

GLOOM
Leandro

We argue—should we track the puma to her den
and observe her cubs to make sure
she's feeding them,
or should we let nature
be natural?

I want to let my dog figure out where the cubs are.
Ana thinks we should wait and see what happens.
The light between us turns blue, then purple,
no way to reclaim
brightness.

Ana is usually the one who wants to think of the puma
as her friend, but somehow we've switched sides.
I'm not willing to wait for wildlife biologists
to meet, discuss, plan, and decide
how to handle this crisis.

There was a time in Florida
when a litter of panther cubs got separated
from their mother, and it took three days
for her to find them,
but what if this time
it takes longer—
won't newborns
starve?

SINKING

Leandro

When I finally go home
unable to sleep,
all I see is a wave
in waking dreams
over and over,
    the rolling barrel
           perfect for surfing
               each drop of water
burnished with reflections
of drowned faces
inside.

Panic in a Daydream

Leandro

no different than awake
except I can't faint, my pulse swirls
I sway in circles
vertigo
lying down
and yet
somehow
stillness too
as I move
through
imaginary
depths
slowly
floating
my lungs
no longer
struggling
I've already reached
the deep seafloor's
silence

IRIDESCENT

Ana

The argument was stupid. Neither of us knows
what to do. We just need to wait for experts to decide
instead of letting our brightness
turn shadowy.

I haven't cried in months,
not since I was homeless,
but now each tear flows
glistening
rainbow colors
trapped
inside
each
drop.

Cielo the singing dog

if only humans understood nature
their minds of air and scent
would never
give up

so I sniff
along the surface of dirt
tracing the wild aroma of cat
even though my real task
is matchmaking
heart-guiding
finding
fixing
lost
love

WILDLIFE DETECTION
Leandro

Cielo finds four cubs
alone in a rocky refuge
surrounded by boulders
and caverns.

The babies look like toys,
their fur spotted and eyes blue,
the tawny gold of adult pumas
not yet developed.

As soon as I see them, I know
that I've made a mistake—they're alone
but probably just for a moment.

What if the mother returns and attacks us?
I should have waited for experts, instead of
always struggling
to prove that I'm brave.

INDECISION

Ana

Leandro went without me.
He didn't wait for us to agree.

It feels like a betrayal.
Should I confront him angrily
or just quietly report him to Art
and the wildlife biology
conservation dog team
even if it means
that he'll be
disqualified
from training?

I can't decide.
So I roam the nursery
gathering seeds, which I label
in tiny envelopes, creating
a Little Free Library of growth
so that gardeners can reach in
and gather handfuls
of possibility.

Puma News from All over California

Leandro

Back at home, I hide in my room, searching
all sorts of articles that pop up from projects I follow.
M-317 has been wandering around homes
in Orange County, returning over and over
each time he's moved.

In the Santa Cruz Mountains
so many pumas have been killed by cars
that a forested tunnel beneath Highway 17
is just about to begin construction.

P-65 and two cubs were observed crossing
Highway 101 in Los Angeles, not far from a place
where the world's largest wildlife bridge
will soon be built, the groundbreaking ceremony
scheduled for Earth Day
wildflower season
a time of hope.

WILD THOUGHTS
Leandro

I need a wilderness crossing
inside my mind, to carry me
away from

                                    worries.

Together

Ana

Valentine's Day.
We forgive each other.
You bake a dulce de leche cake
decorated with caramelized flowers
of every color, edible pansies, a symbol
of thought, la rosa blanca for peace,
and marigolds, which represent light.

Veils of sugar
above petals
like a mist
seen from
        the lighthouse.

        We still need to make a decision.
        No one else knows where the cubs are,
but it will have to wait until morning
because for tonight our shared
radiance
is enough. . . .

Discovery

Ana

Under the bench near the front door of the cottage
Cielo finds two blue-eyed puma cubs
just as Leandro is leaving.

Caona must have brought them, carried the way
all cats carry kittens, one at a time, neck held by jaws
that know how
to be gentle.

Instantly, both cubs curl around the dog,
treating her like a littermate.

Waiting
Leandro

We can't leave the cubs
alone . . .

but we're running the risk that their mother
might return with the other two and find my dog
cuddling as if she's a puma.

So I call Art to make a Wildlife Incident Report,
and then we wait, holding hands, Ana's fingers
and mine pulsing with light as we focus
all our attention
on hope.

Cielo the singing dog

as if the kittens
are my own
puppies
I hum
a lullaby
of courage

We Call the Experts

Ana

I've already named the two puma kittens
secretly, inside my mind—Karaya and Güey
because the spotted fur of one is moon-pale
and the other is sun-hued, like their mother.

Leandro and I are almost adults.
Everything that seemed so impossible
a few months ago
now begins to feel real.

College.
Careers.
Freedom from fear.
The courage to make our own decisions.
All we need is a few more hours of waiting for help
and then a few years of education
and experience.

So we wait.
By the time wildlife biologists arrive,
it's clear that Caona isn't coming back in a hurry.

DEADLINE

Leandro

Maybe in the morning
the mother puma will come
to claim her cubs.

But no, one whole day
passes and half of another
before finally the hungry babies
have to be rescued.

They're crated and taken to the Oakland Zoo,
where they'll be cared for by keepers who have
already saved many orphaned pumas.

All Cielo, Ana, and I can do is visit later,
when the cubs are healthy, after veterinarians
treat them for dehydration, malnutrition,
and rodenticide poisoning.

It's not an ending.
This is their beginning.

EARTH DAY

Leandro and Ana

The rewilding club takes a field trip
to the groundbreaking ceremony
for the world's largest wildlife crossing,
a vegetated bridge above ten lanes of traffic
on Highway 101, near Los Angeles.

A genetic island in city parks will be connected
with the Santa Monica Mountains, so that pumas
can find mates and have healthy babies . . .

but on the day before the ceremony,
P-97 is killed by a car on the nearby 405,
so everyone at the groundbreaking
feels an emotional blend of loss
and determination.

It's a beginning,
not an ending.

Imagine a time when there are wildlife crossings
over or under every highway on Earth.

Cielo the singing dog

their hands touch
as they stand close
beginning the rest
of their lives
light
love

Author's Note

After writing *Your Heart, My Sky* and *Wings in the Wild*, I wanted to pursue one more young adult love story about teenagers who are rediscovering the natural world and their place in it. *Wild Dreamers* is fiction, but all the puma incidents are real, including strolls through beach towns in daytime and the abandonment of cubs by starving mothers.

Personal experience played a role in the writing of this novel. I was briefly homeless as a teenager, and I have always been terrified of ocean waves. I have panic attacks on airplanes, and several family members have the type of panic attack that can cause fainting, but they are brave people who will actively rescue others whenever danger is present.

When I was growing up in Los Angeles, there were pet shops that sold captive pumas—also called mountain lions or cougars—as curiosities. The State of California paid a bounty for each puma killed by a hunter. More recently, I have seen paw prints while hiking in foothills, and I've heard the chirp-like cry of a mother calling to her cubs, followed by a yowl to warn strangers away from her den. I've seen warning signs in rewilded parks near San Francisco, where pumas often show up on doorbell video cameras. Tracks near my semi-rural home near Fresno were identified by wildlife biologists as puma.

California's pumas are divided into ten "genetic islands" separated by traffic. On Earth Day 2022, ground was broken for the world's largest wildlife crossing, the Wallis Annenberg Wildlife Crossing near Los Angeles, which will connect urban and Santa Monica Mountain pumas.

When I decided to write about rewilded habitats and wildlife connectivity in California, the main characters emerged as Cuban Americans. I hope you enjoy discovering Ana, Leandro, and the singing dog Cielo, who learns how to be a conservation dog as well as a companion and matchmaker.

Acknowledgments

I thank God for nature. I'm grateful to my family and friends for their encouragement. For information, I'm indebted to the following organizations: California Native Plant Society, California Mountain Lion Project, Canines for Conservation, the Golden Gate National Recreation Area, the George Wright Society, Latino Outdoors, and numerous rewilding projects all over the world.

Special thanks to my wonderful agent, Michelle Humphrey; author and authenticity reader Mark Oshiro; my amazing editor, Reka Simonsen; assistant editor Kristie Choi; designer Rebecca Syracuse; managing editor Kaitlyn San Miguel; and the whole superb Atheneum publishing team.